Poly Jolly Christmas: A Spicy Holiday Romance

Giselle Renarde

Published by Giselle Renarde, 2022.

First Ebook 2010

Second Edition 2022

Previously published as "All the Way" by Excessica Publishing

Poly Jolly Christmas

A Spicy Holiday Romance
by
Giselle Renarde

Chapter One

"I just don't understand why he'd *want* to spend the holidays with us," Rob said. Setting down his watercolour brush, he followed Josie into the bedroom. It's not that he minded houseguests, but why *Kaz* of all people? "Doesn't he have a family of his own?"

"Of course he has a family," Josie replied as she kicked her shoes under the bed. "But his mother moved to Japan last year and his father isn't the most amiable guy on the planet. Anyway, his parents never really celebrated Christmas and he's feeling kind of low right now. I figured the invitation would brighten his mood."

"Well, I guess it did, if he accepted." Leaning against the doorframe, Rob watched Josie strip out of her office clothes.

Her grey jacket came off to settle on their neatly made bed before the matching skirt fell to the floor. As she unbuttoned her ruffled pink shirt, Rob picked up the suit and hung it in the closet. *Wrinkles now means ironing later.*

When she leaned in to toss her blouse in the laundry hamper, the soft scent of her perfume melted away his haughty mood. Her breasts basked in her ivory lace bra like chocolate ice cream in filigree bowls. The curve of her belly led his eyes to matching panties, which gave that same gorgeous impression of light fabric against dark skin.

All Rob had to do was take one look at his beautiful wife to know he'd give her anything she wanted. *You want your high school boyfriend to stay at our house for Christmas? Sure! No arguments here.*

Placing her arms around his neck, she asked, "Are you sure you're good with this? There's still time to retract if you're not."

When he considered the number of transient artists and acquaintances he'd brought home over the years, he figured it was only fair.

Rolling his hands around her luscious backside, he replied, "I guess if Kaz needs a good boost, *Casa Josie* is the best place for it around the holidays."

"Damn sure!" A huge smile grew across her lips right before she pounced, tickling his neck. "Here, we celebrate Christmas like nobody's business."

In a fit of giddiness, he said, "We celebrate like a house on fire!"

"We celebrate like it's 1999!"

She giggled as he harangued her neck with a mess of silly kisses.

He led her to bed, where they collapsed together in absolute hysterics. When he dug his fingers deep into the flesh of her thighs—the most ticklish spot on her lusciously lovely body—she flipped. Literally. Her reaction was such violent amusement she actually flipped him over, flat on his back. He saw what was coming next in her eyes and in the wicked smile bleeding across her lips, but by the time he reacted it was already too late.

Before he could squeeze his arms tight enough against his sides, her fingers were lodged in his armpits like ten little playground bullies. She pinned him down, laughing her ass off as she tickled his pits. It just about killed him, but it felt good.

It felt *so good* to laugh like that.

He could hardly breathe. His sides ached as he hooted and hollered. Josie was relentless in her attack, but what else was new?

"Let me get that door," she said.

With a familiar glint in her eye, she slipped from the bed. Just as his poor stomach muscles started to relax, Josie closed the bedroom door and they heard a loud *thunk*.

"What was that?" Rob asked. He slid off the bed with the moderated panic of knowing it was either something or nothing.

When she swung the door back open, there stood Froggy with his small hand cradling his forehead. Their child possessed the uncanny ability to succumb to injury with only a stunned sense of wonder about it. He never cried in the face of physical pain.

Josie gazed down at him, frozen in place. She must have pushed the door closed just as the poor little guy came around the corner to run into their bedroom.

With his three-year-old inability to pronounce his *th*, *r*, and *t* sounds, Froggy's manner of expressing that the door had hit him in the head sounded something like, "Da doy hip me in da head," but his meaning was obvious. His insistence on describing the event was for informational purposes only. Froggy *informed*. He did not *complain*.

"Angelfish, are you all right?" Josie cried, falling to her knees before him. "Mommy's sorry. She didn't see you there."

Scooping the boy into his arms, Rob struggled to keep his tone jocular. "We're going to have to put a bell on you, kiddo! Mommy and Daddy didn't hear you coming."

Though, upon reflection, it made perfect sense that Froggy would seek them out when they were causing such a ruckus. He always had to know what people were laughing about, because he always worried they were laughing about him.

"Mommy is so, so sorry, sweety," she repeated, kissing the little hand still propped against his forehead. "How about Mommy gets us all bundled up and we go outside and make a snowman? How about that?"

Froggy reflected for a moment, removing his hand from his head to tap his finger against his lips. He had the look of a little professor as he replied, "Not snow *man*. Make a snow *gigakiki*!"

"Oh, a gigakiki," Josie replied with a big nod.

When she shot Rob an amused glance, he set their son down and said, "I guess you'd better tell Mom what a gigakiki is. I don't think she's ever heard of it before."

Josie pulled on a pair of fleece pants as Froggy explained, "A gigakiki is a big-big-big cat as big as the whole house."

"Wow," she chuckled, crawling into a long-sleeved top and sweater. "Sounds like it's going to take a lot of snow to make one of those."

"Yep," Froggy replied. "A lot a lot."

Scooping him up and carrying him over her shoulder like a bundle of firewood, she said, "Okay, let's get your snowsuit on, young one."

"Enjoy your play time," Rob said, kissing her temple as she passed him by. "While you're out there, you can start thinking if there's anything special you want for Christmas dinner. I'd rather pick it up before the store get too-too packed."

"Oh, didn't I tell you?" Spinning on a dime, Josie nearly whacked Froggy's head against the doorframe. She stepped away just in time, but it was a noticeable near miss. "Jeez," she hissed, turning to look at Froggy, whose face was quite close to hers. "Sorry, my little one. Mommy's got to take it easy, doesn't she?"

"Mommy's got to take it easy," he repeated with a nod.

"Tell me what?" Rob asked.

"What?"

"What were you going to tell me about dinner?"

"Oh," she replied, setting Froggy down. "Go find your hat and mitts, okay?"

He didn't budge, of course, but she didn't seem to notice.

"Just that my sister invited us for Christmas dinner."

With some trepidation, Rob inquired, "*Which* sister?"

"Oh. Adrianna."

Froggy cheered, "Yes!" and turned side to side, punching the air in all directions. This was his happy dance. "I get to play with cousin Ben! I get to play with cousin Ben!"

Rob considered how much he looked forward to preparing Christmas dinner, leading up to the big day. Then he always resented the task when everybody else was spreading good cheer and he was stuck in the kitchen. "Actually, that sounds not half bad. Adrianna's a great cook. Sweet of her to invite us."

Her brown eyes sparkled with hints of gold as she shot him a grateful smile. "You go get some work done, cutie. We'll get out of your hair for a while."

Picking Froggy up again, she zoomed him like a rocket ship down the stairs and into the front hall, where her jacket and his snowsuit awaited them.

Chapter Two

"When are we going to Auntie's?" Froggy asked, fidgeting endlessly as Josie pushed his little foot into the snowsuit.

"On Christmas," she replied, kissing his button nose. "Are you excited? I'm excited."

"I'm excited," he repeated.

When she'd finished bundling him head to toe, she slipped on her jacket and opened the door to the winter wonderland that was their front yard. During the summer months, it was all burnt patches of lawn, dandelions and crabgrass. Endless worry about which varieties of flora would survive in the shade of the maple tree. In the winter, Nature took care of all of that. She covered the lawn with a blanket of cashmere snow and there was nothing to worry about. It was lovely.

"Mommy," Froggy said in a scolding sort of voice. "Where do you think you're going with no hat?"

She tried not to smile, but she couldn't help it. His concern was adorable. Running her fingers through her mess of curls, she replied, "Mommy's hair is too sticky-up-y for a hat. How about she just wears ear warmers instead?"

"*And* mittens," he insisted.

"And mittens," she agreed. Of course, she couldn't find a matching pair in the big box of winter gear. She settled on one bright pink ski glove and one black woollen mitten with a sprig of holly embroidered on the back.

When they'd found the perfect spot for a gigakiki and started to build it tail-first, Froggy asked, "How many days until Christmas?"

Josie counted them off on the fingers of her gloved hand, since she couldn't see the ones inside her mitten. "Christmas Eve is tomorrow, and the next day is Christmas. How many days is that?"

They counted her fingers together. "One, two."

Froggy shook with excitement. He danced around the base of the gigakiki, shouting, "Two more days 'til Christmas. Two more days 'til Christmas!"

Josie could feel his enthusiasm running through her body. With that reminiscence of childlike joy, she fell into the snow and flailed her arms and legs in the cool whiteness.

"Snow angels!" Froggy cried, running to join her. When they rose to examine their creations, he said, "It's a mommy angel and a Froggy angel."

"Yes it is," she replied, casting her gaze toward the sidewalk. The neighbours four doors down trudged by with their Saint Bernard. She nodded, but they didn't say hello.

Maybe it was time to clear a better path.

"How about your mommy angel shovels some snow while you finish the gigakiki?"

Froggy stared up at her for a moment, his lower lip hanging open a tad. Any other child would whine and complain. Froggy simply said, "Okay," and picked up more snow to add to his giant cat.

Relieved by his cool reaction, Josie went into the garage to fetch a shovel.

Is it strange, she asked herself as she cleared a path across sidewalk, *that Kaz wants to stay for Christmas?*

After all, it wasn't like they were close buddies or anything. He was on her instant messenger list, along with about thirty other people. They only really scratched the surface any time they chatted online.

She'd only started chatting with him in the first place because her workday became insufferable around three in the afternoon. He always seemed to be online.

Josie froze in the middle of the sidewalk as another thought occurred to her: *Does Rob think we're having an affair?*

Josie looked at the individual pieces: old boyfriend, increased contact, a holiday invitation out of the blue, not to mention all the overtime she'd been putting in at work lately. If Rob was looking to mistrust her, the pieces certainly added up to adultery.

Like I would ever!

Kaz was a cute boy, but he never made her bra boil over and her panties melt into a pool of passion. She didn't even have sex with him when they were together. She was hardly going to start now.

"Mommy angel," a familiar little voice called out from beside an ever-increasing snow cat.

"Yes, Froggy angel?"

Placing his hands on the hips of his snowsuit, he scolded, "You stopped working."

She found it amusing how children committed to a task and expected the same of the adults in their care.

"I'm sorry, little one," she replied, trying very hard not to chuckle at his adorableness.

When she got back to work, so did he.

But what was *Kaz* thinking, accepting an invitation she'd only really offered out of a sense of pitying politeness?

He seemed lonely.

Not *seemed*. He said as much: he *was* lonely.

Working and living alone as he did, he didn't get much human interaction into his daily diet. That was a shame, because Kaz had some very interesting things to say whenever anybody gave him the opportunity.

Unfortunately, Kaz always seemed to draw in people with big mouths. Josie had been one of those people, when they first met. She only gave him a chance to speak in the first place because they were paired up in science lab and she thought—very misguidedly, as it turned out—that she wasn't any good with STEM.

Though their relationship hadn't been hot and heavy, it was a turning point in Josie's life. Kaz brought out her inner girl-geek, and helped her embrace a love of numbers that most young women repressed in want of fitting in.

She was beyond indebted to him for that.

It was Kaz who set her on the path to a thriving career in statistical analysis. Without the proceeds from that career, there was no way Rob could stay home with Froggy and work at his first love.

Her husband was a very talented artist and an expert illustrator, but his career didn't exactly bring in the big bucks.

As she scraped at the impertinent ice beneath the snow, a long-lost voice behind her said, "Josie? Is that you?"

"Whoa," she cried, nearly jumping out of her snow boots as she turned to see who'd come up behind her. "Kaz! You scared me half to death."

She could have sworn he used to have an accent, but he didn't anymore. And he looked so... *cool!* There was no other word to describe his indie hairstyle and his weathered jeans and old cord jacket.

Wrapping her arms around the guy who looked nothing like he did in her memory, Josie rambled, "Don't you dare team up with my son! You're both quiet as mice. You'll drive us nuts."

"Josie," he repeated as she released him from a gentle hug. Glancing down at her mismatched mittens, he said, "You look better than ever."

She bit the inside of her lip to keep from smiling too widely. "Shut up," she giggled, pushing him away like high school girl. "No I don't."

Josie couldn't get over how great he looked. He'd been such a nerd in school. Now he was the kind of guy she'd definitely go up to in a club... if she weren't happily married, of course.

"That's weird," he said, brushing snow out of her hair.

"Oh, we were making snow angels."

"No, I mean our hair colour," he replied, lifting the strap of his backpack.

"Oh yeah. We used to both have black hair, now we both have orangey highlights. But I guess that's the style, right?"

"Right," he said with a bashful smile. "You always were the practical one."

"Hardly," she chuckled as Froggy approached. He circled once around Josie's legs before she stopped him by setting her hand on his head. "I'd like you to meet a little someone. This is my son Ewan."

"No, tell him *Froggy*," her son said in a loud whisper.

As Kaz sank to his knees, she relented, "I'm sorry. We *named* him Ewan, but he prefers to be called Froggy."

Once Kaz was at eye level with the boy, he said, "It's great to meet you, Froggy. My parents named me Kazuhiro, but I like it better when people call me Kaz. That means you and I have something in common, and *that* means we can be friends."

Froggy smiled, but looked quickly up at Josie for confirmation. She and Rob were vigilant about the *don't talk to strangers* rule. Smiling back at her son, she confirmed, "My friend Kaz is going to stay with us over Christmas. I'm just going to run in the house for a sec. Why don't you show our guest the gigakiki?"

As she skirted past Kaz, she noticed the wheeled suitcase he'd been dragging behind him. "Oh, let me take that in the house for you."

"That's okay, Jos," he replied.

Just like Rob, he called her *Jos*.

She gulped hard, snatching the handle away from him. "Don't be silly. I'm going into the house. I insist."

With a gushing smile, he agreed.

Pulling his suitcase up the driveway, Josie perched her shovel against the garage door, and carried the big bag inside. The second she'd closed the door, she dropped it and ran to the front window. "Rob," she called out in the loudest whisper she could muster. She didn't want to risk Kaz hearing, even from outside. "Rob, come here for a sec."

Rob came in from the kitchen, wiping his hands on a tea towel. "What's up?"

"He's here," she said, pointing out the window to the hot guy helping Froggy build a bigger, better, and more realistic gigakiki. "Kaz is here already."

"*That's* Kaz? I thought you said he was a lonely nerd."

"He was!"

The look on her husband's face said he obviously didn't believe her.

"He *was*. If he looked like that back in the day, do you think I would have dumped him? Anyway," she went on without letting Rob get a word in. "What he looks like isn't the point. The point is that he's here. *Now*. I wasn't expecting him until tomorrow afternoon."

"You mean he showed up early? That was pretty rude of the dude." Rob twisted the tea towel and slapped it against his hand like a riding crop. Putting on an accent, he joked, "Ve have vays of dealing viss his sort."

Josie couldn't help laughing as her husband pranced about the family room like a German dominatrix. "You're crazy, you know that?"

"Zat is vy you love me."

Though she turned her attention to the front yard, she could still see Rob wielding his dishtowel-whip in the reflection of the bay window. It was getting dark outside.

"You totally distracted me," she said, trying to shake the image out of her head. "I think I told Kaz to come anytime, and he was welcome to help us decorate the tree tomorrow. I worded it like that."

"Open to interpretation," Rob stated. When he snapped his whip again, it hit their framed Waterhouse print, knocking it off-kilter. He looked at her with the sheepish expression even Froggy had outgrown. Chuckling nervously, he set the picture frame straight, and then took his tea towel back to the kitchen. "Time to put this thing away, I guess."

As she opened the front door to call Kaz and Froggy inside, Rob hissed.

Josie ran to the kitchen only to find him staring with despair into a big pot on the stove.

"I forgot I was making hot chocolate. The real kind, with cocoa and milk."

"Oh," Josie replied, one eye on the door as her son led her old boyfriend in from the cold. "I'm sure it'll be fine if you give it a stir."

A panicked surge raced through her as she realized Kaz and Rob would soon be in the same room together. The image of her husband and her high school sweetheart duking it out in a sumo ring flashed before her eyes, and she gasped for air. *I really haven't thought this out, have I?*

"It might be salvageable," Rob called from the kitchen.

"Good, great," she replied absently.

As she knelt to help Froggy with his winter boots, she heard Rob's footfall. When she looked up, she realized she'd managed to plant her face three inches from Kaz's crotch—and right at eye level, too!

Her throat let out a high-pitched *eep*, but he stepped out of his ultra-cool leather boots without seeming to notice.

She turned her head to see Rob setting down a tray of mugs in the living room.

"Honey," she said, bolting upright with Froggy's boots in hand.

They both turned. With the male gaze resting squarely on Josie, she suddenly felt like her clubhouse was full of boys.

"Rob, this is Kaz," she introduced, though they probably would have figured out who was who. "Kaz, Rob."

"Yeah, we actually met at your wedding," Kaz replied, eying the sofa and drinks.

"Oh, that's right," Josie said. "I totally forgot."

"Please, sit down," Rob motioned. "I made hot chocolate."

At the sound of those two magical words, Froggy shouted, "Hot chocolate! Hot chocolate!" and ran for his cup.

"Go slow, Froggy-angel. It's hot," Josie warned, setting his mittens on the radiator to dry.

"I guess I burned it a smidge," Rob apologized as Kaz reached for a mug. "Sorry if it's a little off."

"No, it's great," Kaz replied. "Burning stuff brings out the caramel taste in the sugars. That's why you burn crème brulé, right?"

As they conversed about cooking with the ease of old friends, it dawned on Josie that there were only three mugs of hot chocolate in total. Josie, Rob, and Froggy made three. He hadn't counted on Kaz arriving early. And she knew Rob; she knew he'd let her have the third.

What a sweetheart.

Picking up the last mug, she passed it to her husband, who simply shook his head and said, "It's for you."

She watched her surroundings, feeling oddly estranged from them. Froggy blew on his cup as Rob and Kaz talked about recipe websites. After a few sips of deliciously creamy hot chocolate, she passed the mug to Rob. "We'll share, babe."

When he smiled at her, she felt so at ease that she teased herself for having trepidations. There was nothing strange about any of this.

"You know, I've got to say, I don't remember you from our wedding," Rob began. "Most of our friends aren't so cool. I'm sure I would have remembered you."

Josie could have laughed out loud. *Rob has a man-crush!*

"Trust me, I was *not* very memorable back then," Kaz replied. "Just your run-of-the-mill computer nerd. I still am, at heart. My old girlfriend just fixed up the package a bit."

"I bet she did," Rob chuckled, with a furtive glance in Froggy's direction.

Froggy was fine, still exploring the cosmos in a cup.

Kaz offered a forced smile. "Right, well, she made me more to her liking, mainly so I wouldn't embarrass her around her friends."

"That's kind of funny," Josie cut in. "Well, not *funny*, but you know what I mean. Because that's the exact opposite of what you did for me. You helped me find my inner girl geek and be proud of her."

Just as she was beginning to feel sublimely cosy, Froggy looked up at her and said, "I'm hungry."

"Oh, that's right. We haven't eaten dinner," she said, suppressing that mean little voice scolding, *For shame! Must your son remind you to feed him?*

With their newfound discovery of each other's penchants for cooking, Rob and Kaz went nuts with dinner ideas. After digging through cupboards and flipping through cookbooks, they reached the consensus that, even if they had all the right ingredients, it was already too late to start preparing a nice coq-au-vin or anything along those lines.

The pair of tongue-teasers got Josie's taste buds all riled up for haute cuisine, but ultimately gave up and ordered pizza.

After story time with Mommy, Daddy, and their new best friend Kaz, Froggy was out like a light and Josie could finally decompress. As much as she'd enjoyed playing in the snow and catching up with an old friend, she needed some alone time with her hubby. He so often went without, when she worked those extra hours.

A surge of joy ran through her at the thought of a few days off.

"On holiday—finally!" she squealing, hugging Rob around the neck as he bent low to stack the dishwasher. "Hey, what would you say to opening up the hot tub and going for a soak?"

"That sounds great!" Kaz replied, patting them both on the shoulders. "I didn't bring a bathing suit or anything but, hey, we're all grown-ups, right?"

Chapter Three

Josie was about to give Kaz a friendly swat and say, *Very funny, mister.*

She only had to take one look at him to see that he wasn't joking.

"Oh," she stammered. "Well, you know, the hot tub's outside. Most people can't stand the thought of braving the snow in their skivvies, so if you'd rather not, we would totally *totally* understand."

"Are you kidding?" Kaz asked, bubbling over with a seductive sort of glee. "That sounds like the perfect way to sit back, relax, and really get to know each other."

Glancing sheepishly at Josie, Rob replied, "Yeah, it certainly can be."

"I just realized what a rude jerk I am!" Kaz cried, smacking his forehead with his hand. Just as Josie started breathing a sigh of relief, he walked to the front hall and said, "I left my luggage sitting here like it's going to grow legs and walk itself to my room. Please, let me get all this crap out of your way."

Josie and Rob breathed a collective sigh before Rob said, "Why don't I show you to the guest room while Josie checks the chlorine levels in the tub."

"*Bromine*," she called, shaking her head as Rob led Kaz to the guest room. He never listened when it came to practical matters. "Put chlorine into the mix and the whole tub will explode."

The night was even milder than she'd anticipated: one of those rare states after the snow stopped falling and before the temperature dropped and the winds picked up. There wasn't even a breeze out as she brushed fresh snow off the tub cover.

When she lifted the top, stream rose up to the sky. It was deep, dark, inky blue pierced by pinholes of starlight.

As she breathed the fresh night air into her lungs, the light clicked on in the guest room. It suddenly occurred to her how fortunate they were to have everything they did, and how great it was to be able to share their bounty with others.

She really didn't resent Kaz staying with them, or showing up earlier than anticipated, or even invite himself into the tub. It's not like she deserved these things any more than anybody else.

The pH and temperature were pretty close to perfect, so, with a few minor adjustments, she headed upstairs to jump into her suit. She could hear the deep vibration of the men's voices up in the attic room.

The one-piece or the bikini?

Daring as it seemed, she chose the turquoise two-piece lined in chocolate brown.

As she suited up, a racket like a herd of college boys shook the house. If she didn't know better, she'd have thought it was an earthquake.

Darting to the bedroom door, she threw it open just in time to see a naked Kaz racing down the attic staircase like a kid on Christmas morning. Rob was close behind, just as naked and twice as giddy. He stopped at the linen closet as Kaz kept on to the ground floor.

Josie didn't process the scene fast enough to be shocked by it. Instead, she went straight to giggles. Their adorably juvenile behaviour reminded her of the time in high school when Kaz and his buddy Paul skipped fourth-period to perch their asses outside the classroom window, mooning everybody inside.

Even nerdy boys acted like maniacs sometimes.

"How's the tub?" Rob asked, tossing her a towel as he followed Kaz downstairs. "Can we get in now?"

Sucking her teeth, she teased, "You'd better get your filthy asses into that hot water. Last thing I want is you two sitting your buck naked selves down on my good furniture."

She laughed at her own jokes even after the sliding glass door opened and the boys coursed into the backyard. Before heading down, she peeked into Froggy's room to find his angelic eyelids resting closed like waxy little rose petals. *How could that child sleep through such racket?*

She leaned in to kiss his forehead before closing his door to join the naked men outside.

Josie ran across the deck in flip-flops, kicking them off as she threw her towel over the cleared deck chair.

The cold didn't even manage to catch her up before she slipped her skin beneath the warm water. It bubbled away like a witch's brew as she leaned into the jets next to Rob. She reached for his hand as he reached for hers, and they found each other's thighs instead, which was just as good.

Kaz sat across from them, which seemed fortuitous. Even together in the same hot bubbles, they could get away with murder under the hydric hum of the tub.

"Your head's not too cold?" Rob called to Kaz over the noise.

"Huh?" he replied, placing a hand behind his ear. "I can't hear you."

"Perfect," Rob whispered to Josie as he slipped his fingers between her legs.

Kaz shrugged and closed his eyes, at one with his jets. His seat was roughly the same as hers, with water flows attacking the stress in her lower back, upper back, mid back, not to mention her butt.

The one thing Kaz didn't have was a husband's naughty fingers creeping under turquoise bathing bottoms. The wetness that dear hubby came across was more than just water. It was the very nectar of Josie's lust for him.

She couldn't very well mount her man with Kaz across the way, even if his eyes were closed. What she *could* do was squirm out of her bottoms and hold them tight in one hand while she worked her way down to Rob's cock with the other hand.

His hardness made her gasp—or perhaps that was the fingers slowly stroking her clit.

Though she tried not to make much noise while he played with her pussy, her cries wouldn't make much difference over the jets. She took a firm hold of his cock, rubbing up to the tip until she could feel that skin-on-skin sensation she loved so much.

Handjobs were fun, both giving and getting. She opened her legs wide, tossing her thigh over Rob's as he snuck a wayward finger into her slit. As he penetrated her, she set his cock against her outer thigh and gave it a good smack. Rob loved that; she could see it in his eyes.

He reached deep inside her to rub that sweet spot marked with a *g* and Josie went wild.

Pressing his palm flat against her clit, he rubbed it in circles. Josie almost felt guilty. There was no way what she was doing to him even half equaled the pleasure he was giving her.

Wrapping her fist around his cockhead, she teased the tip alone, pulling it while she cupped it in her hand. Rob liked being hard in her hands. He liked the pressure and the jerking. She liked it too. She liked the rubbing feeling inside her body, compounded by the swirling motion on her clit as he stroked it in circles.

Her pleasure mounted as she watched the enjoyment on his face. His lips formed the words *I love you* before he threw his head back in ecstasy. He held on tight to her pussy, like he'd caught her with a curiously finger-like fish hook.

She writhed against his static hold, never letting go of his cock as she ground her pussy against his hand. His palm on her clit felt so good-beyond-good she couldn't contain herself.

Just as a wayward cry escaped her lips, the hot tub clicked and she knew she had to shut her mouth because the bubbles were going to stop in three... two... one...

Silence.

Chapter Four

Kaz opened his eyes wide the way Froggy did when he thought he'd inadvertently broken something. Rob must have noticed his terror, because he said, "Don't panic. The jet cycle just ended."

Josie suppressed a chuckle as her husband rolled his head in orgasmic circles. He looked like a bobble-head doll.

"Want me to turn the bubbles back on?" she asked Kaz. "All it takes is the push of a button."

"No, that's okay," he replied, shifting into the deep seat beside her. It didn't seem like a big deal until she realized he was naked and she was sitting on her bathing suit bottoms. How could she squirm back into them without him noticing?

Although, in the dark, did it really matter?

Chuckling, Kaz looked over to Rob and said, "Whoa, man, I think you might like those jets a little too much."

Josie let out a weird high-pitched laugh as Rob set his head on her shoulder. "Yeah, he'd have married this tub if he'd met it first."

"Maybe if you'd met *him* first you would have married *me*, right?" Kaz gurgled, sticking his toes out of the water at the opposite end of the tub.

The question made Josie's spine straighten. That was *exactly* the kind of thing she didn't want to get into.

"Who knows?" she said with that same high-pitched laugh.

"Take her, she's yours," Rob murmured as if in a dream.

With a giggle of surprise, she teased him with a playful slap to the chest. "Think you can go passing your wife around?"

Hugging her, Rob replied, "It's okay. I'm done with you. I'm ready to move on."

"Like hell you are," she laughed.

"I had a girlfriend," Kaz broke in. His tone seemed sad.

Josie could feel Rob inhaling sharply as he sat up. The still water shifted around him. It was the sound of an oar in a midnight lake.

"Yeah, I remember you mentioning that," Josie said. She would have set her hand on his thigh if she knew she could get there on target.

"Do you want to know why she broke up with me?"

"Why was that?" Rob asked, petting Josie's leg. She always felt so lucky when other people talked about losing love. It wasn't a sense of *schadenfreude*; it was more like delight in knowing she had someone as great as Rob to share her life with. She recognized how rare that was.

"There were a lot of reasons," Kaz began. "Sure, she fixed me up, aesthetically. I looked really cool, but I was still a nerd. She kept trying to make me into something else, but we are what we are, you know?"

"Yup," Josie replied, smiling at all the memories flooding back. "That's what you told me when you realized I was smart. I didn't want anyone to know. Smart and cool didn't go together."

Disturbing the water in front of him, Kaz said, "It wasn't just that you didn't want anyone else to know—you didn't even want *yourself* to know."

She smiled, realizing her eyes had adjusted to the light of the moon and stars. Kaz smiled back for a moment, but his expression became forlorn again as he said, “The other thing about my old girlfriend was that I always came in her hands.”

Rob sputtered, like he was choking on a drink. “Whoa, too much information, man!”

“Oh, shut up, Rob.” She smacked his wet chest. “What, are you stuck in the 90’s or something? *Too much information...*”

“Yeah,” Kaz went on, unperturbed. “Would you believe I’m still a virgin? All the years Shelley and I were together, I never got inside her. Not once. There were times when she’d get out a condom and by the time she’d rolled it down, I’d already filled the damn thing with jizz.”

“Dude,” Rob said, with a note of mockery in his voice. Josie pinched him and he straightened up to say, “That’s too bad, man. But I guess she wanted something you weren’t.”

“Yeah,” Josie picked up. “If she couldn’t take you for who you are, you probably weren’t meant to be together.”

“I know,” Kaz acknowledged. “Honestly, I always felt like I needed a really special girl to lose my virginity to. Josie, I still think that girl is you.”

Oh God.

The steam rising from the tub choked her as she struggled to get air in her lungs. She stared straight ahead, unable to succumb to the pressure of looking either her husband or her old boyfriend in the eye.

It’s not that she was looking to have an affair or anything. Far from it. She was, for the most part, deliriously happy with married life. It was just... well, she felt so sorry for Kaz.

Maybe if she'd been ready to share her body with a guy back when they were together, he wouldn't be in this situation now.

Rob was the first to speak. "Wow, man. That's a bold thing to admit in front of a girl's husband."

"Yeah, I know," Kaz replied. The men looked around her to meet each other's gazes. "But I wouldn't have said it *not* in front of you, you know what I mean? That's not right." To Josie, he said, "I never brought this up behind his back, right? I never let on I felt that way."

"No, you sure didn't," Josie answered.

She probably wouldn't have invited him to stay for the holidays if he had.

Sitting in the hot tub between the two men, Josie felt like a child strapped into the middle seat of an old car, squished between her mom and her grandmother.

"Excuse me," Josie said, nearly rising out of her seat before she'd put her bottoms back on. After struggling into them quick as a bunny, she hopped up on the side of the tub and down onto the deck. "You guys stay out as long as you please, but I'm..."

As she spoke, she realized she'd put her bottoms on inside out and she hadn't put her flip-flops back on at all. The snow burned her feet.

She left her towel on the chair and raced into the house, embarrassed by the immaturity of her reaction.

When she arrived in the master bedroom, she sat down wet before the mirror just to look herself in the eye.

The jets came back on in the tub, but she didn't budge.

So much could happen, if she let it.

Chapter Five

When Rob came into the bedroom, Josie was still at the mirror, wearing her inside-out bathing suit.

"We're all pruny!" he teased, tickling her neck with waterlogged fingers.

She brushed them away a little harder than he deserved. "Oh, *we* are, are we? Who's *we*?" She didn't give him the opportunity to answer. "And what have *we* been doing all this time?"

He shook his head. "What are you talking about?"

When she looked up at him, she felt tears welling in her eyes.

Kneeling beside her vanity stool, Rob threw his head in her lap.

She watched her expression soften in the mirror.

"I don't know," she replied. "I've been up here thinking what you might say about me, what kind of deal you men would cut with me as chattel. Maybe you'd trade me off in exchange for a good noodle recipe."

"What?" He chuckled softly, adjusting the towel around his middle. "Do you not realize how silly that sounds?"

"Yes," she admitted.

"Josie, honey, you make way more money than I do. Even if I did trade you for noodles, you could easily buy your way out of the purchase agreement."

"I know," she laughed. "And still, I depend on you. It isn't money I come home to at the end of the day. Not even a house. I come home to *you* and this little family. If you weren't here, I would..." The images scratching like beetles across her heart were so horrific she had to repress them even before their veils had lifted. "I need you."

"I need you too," Rob said, nodding in her lap. "I wouldn't trade you for all the noodle recipes in China."

"What about Japan?"

"Throw in Korea and I'd be tempted," he joked. "No, I wouldn't sell you to Kaz. All we were doing in the hot tub was trying to get his cock under control."

As she threw her head back, laughing out loud, a chill breezed across her skin. "Oh, let me up, will you? I need to throw on a sweater or something."

"You shouldn't laugh," he called as she tossed her bathing suit over the towel bar.

Slipping into her super-soft terry robe, she picked up her toothbrush.

Rob came to join her, hanging his towel over the shower rail. Almost in a whisper, he said, "Your man Kaz is really sensitive about the whole premature ejaculation thing."

As he sauntered naked from the bathroom, Josie brushed her teeth and puzzled through what he'd just said.

With her toothbrush hanging out the side of her mouth, she asked, "What are you talking about?"

He jammed his feet into Christmas tree sleep pants and dove like a child into bed. "Oh, you know," he replied, watching her in the open door. "Kaz was just telling me more about that girlfriend situation, and we figured he could do with a lesson in restraint."

Josie stared at her husband as he opened the covers for her. She had *no clue* what he was talking about.

Spitting into the sink, she rinsed her mouth and walked into the bedroom. "I'm missing something, here. What were you doing?"

"Okay," he said as she sat on the bed. "Sometimes a guy has problems holding back when he's with a woman."

"Yeah."

"And when he takes matters into his own hands, everything seems fine. He thinks the problem's solved when he's jackin' it himself, so he goes back to the girl and—*pow!*—he comes in her hands."

"Okay..."

Rob took a big breath before going on. "Sometimes it works to seek help from an outside source."

"Like a sex worker," Josie said. Hell, she was no prude.

"Well, that's what I said, but he says he's never been keen on the idea. So I figure, hey, help a brother out."

"Don't say *brother*." It irked her when white guys talked that way. Still, she couldn't keep herself from smiling at the idea of her husband jerking Kaz off right there in the hot tub. "When you say *help out*, you mean, like, *hands on?*"

"Yeah, and I really think it worked." For a second, his face turned to stone. "Wait, you're okay with all this, right?"

"Yes, yes, yes." She threw off her robe and snuck beneath the covers.

Josie loved the image of her man with a man. She'd always told him she wouldn't consider it cheating if he got with another guy. Hey, guys had parts she didn't. They were altogether different animals. As long as he told her all about it, she was cool as a cucumber.

"So, what did you do? Just jerk him off? You have to tell me *everything*." But before he had a chance to reply, she interrupted him. "Hey, wait... where *is* Kaz?"

"He went up to get his laptop. Did you know that guy has three separate businesses?"

"Yes," she said. "I was there when he told you that. Please, please, please, just tell me what happened. I'm *dying* here!"

After he'd shuffled out of his sleep pants, Rob wrapped his fist around his cock. "I told him to imagine I was a pretty girl while I did this to him. I told him to feel how soft my skin was, and imagine red polish on my nails."

As Rob squeezed his cock, it grew in his hand. Josie didn't keep measurements or anything, but it seemed like his erections had a magical ability to grow infinitely large.

"I took hold of him like this, and he got huge just like I'm getting huge."

"What about you?" Josie asked, pawing at his belly. She kissed his lips as he stroked his cock. "Did you get huge too?"

"A little bit," he admitted. "But I was still pretty gone from you jerking me off."

"But it turned you on, right?" she asked, planting a trail of kisses down his chest. "Touching another guy's dick and making it all nice and hard must have got you *so* horny."

Rob chuckled as she shuffled under the covers. She placed her hand on top of his and took his cockhead between her lips. When she held his fingers and guided their motion, he gasped.

"Honey, I think the idea of me jerking your friend off is making *you* horny."

"You can say that again." She licked the gourmet quality precum from his tip before swallowing the monster.

Rob arched his back and moaned. That meant she was doing a good job—or, rather, *giving* a good job.

As she pumped in time with his rocking hips, she sucked him like a big 'ol candy cane. She plunged her face on him, thrusting her hips as his fingers reached up to tickle her clit.

"I guess you're taking me all the way home like this," Rob said as she rocked her pussy on his hand.

"Oh, you'd like that, wouldn't you?" Sitting up in bed, she traced her fingers all the way up to his cockhead, and then pressed her palm down on the wet tip.

Just as she threw one leg over him, thunderous footfalls came down the attic stairs.

Their bedroom door burst open.

Josie froze.

She didn't need to turn around to know what had happened.

Rob looked beyond her naked body and hissed, "Kaz, close the door, will you?"

"Dude, I am so sorry!" But instead of slinking sheepishly out of the room, he came inside and closed the door. "I just came down to say goodnight, but I can see you're having a good night without me."

"Yeah, that's right." Shaking off her stupor, Josie rolled off Rob and pulled the bed sheets over her naked breasts.

She chuckled nervously as her gaze slid down Kaz's silk pyjamas. The shining red fabric draped over his limbs gave her an even better idea of his essence than his nudity had. She still couldn't get over how *cool* he'd become.

"Did Rob tell you about...?"

"The hot tub," she said. "It's totally fine."

Kaz took a seat at the foot of their bed. "Trust me, I didn't come here thinking I'd seduce your husband, but he said you were cool with stuff like that."

"I wouldn't say you *seduced* me. I mean, let's be fair," Rob interrupted. "It was a practical matter of cock-training."

Josie smiled at her husband. It was so cute how he'd suddenly come down with a case of *don't-call-me-gay*. One little incident in a hot tub hardly coloured her view of his sexuality. If anything, the incident gave him a heightened sex appeal. She guessed he'd jerked off with guys back in university, but now she knew for sure. It happened in her own backyard.

"If we're talking practicality," Josie chimed in, "why don't you jack off before your dates? I've heard that really helps. That way you don't get too excited and you've got a little more control when you get naked with a girl."

"Oh, yeah?"

"Yeah," she replied. "I thought that was common knowledge. Why is it that girls know more about dicks than guys do?"

Rob said, "It's the plight of the modern woman. You know everything there is to know about dicks except how to grow working ones for yourselves."

"Fuck you," Josie said, smacking his hand away from his adorable face. "Don't get all Freudian on me."

"What? That's the quandary of the information age. We've got all the facts, but we don't know how to use them."

She liked the way Kaz looked at her, with a combination of adoration and awe. It made her wish she could go back in time and fuck him in high school. Of course, she couldn't make that happen. But there were other options. It's not like he'd died and gone to heaven. He was right there in front of her, sitting on her bed after jacking off with her husband.

The possibilities were endless.

"You know, Rob," she said, never unlocking her gaze from Kaz's. "Maybe you were on to something with that whole cock-training idea."

"Was I?" he asked, like he was stunned to be right for once.

"Yeah," she replied, letting the covers fall to her hips.

She watched Kaz's gaze swerve to her bare tits, then back up to her eyes. He smiled, but she raised an eyebrow. They were co-conspirators, but not to Rob's exclusion.

"Maybe all Kaz needs is a little experience."

"I know," Rob said. "I think so too."

He shot her a sly smile, and she knew right away he was on board and ready to roll with whatever she had up her sleeve. Not that she was quite sure what that was yet...

"What would help?" she asked, crawling out of the covers and down the mattress. "Do you think it would help if I sucked your cock?"

Rob rolled out of bed to lock the door as Kaz squeaked, "I don't know if I could handle that."

"Sure you could," Rob chimed in, curling back into bed behind Josie. He ran his hands across her ass, giving the closest cheek a loving bite. "Are you concerned about diseases or whatever? Because we're both clean and you're virgin."

"Yeah, thanks for the reminder," Kaz said, gasping as Josie ran her hand along his silky thigh. "I just don't know how long I'll last in a beautiful woman's mouth."

Her heart soared at the compliment.

Finding his cock hard under his silk pyjamas, she replied, "Well, we'll just have to try and find out."

He gasped, tossing his head to his shoulder as she pumped his shaft through his Christmas-red pyjama pants.

"You two are so weird," Kaz said, laughing.

"What do you mean we're weird?" Rob asked as Josie scooped his straining cock into her bare hands.

"Do you do this a lot?" Kaz asked. He spoke in shudders and gasps as Josie played with his cock.

They both laughed, of course. *Did they do this a lot?* What a joke.

"No, we're first-timers," Josie chuckled. She held his shaft steady, then ran her tongue all the way along it, base to tip. When his whole body shook, she worried he was about to blow, so she pinched his drooling cockhead. As his tremors subsided, she clarified: "First-timers when it comes to bringing a third into the bedroom."

"Yeah, we usually only have group sex in the hot tub," Rob teased.

Josie kicked his thigh with her toes. "Pay no attention to the man behind the curtain."

It wasn't true, what they said about Asian guys. Kaz was hung like a stud, and a tingle ran through her as she took his tip between her lips. Instead of lingering or giving little licks all around his rim, she gobbled his cock whole hog.

Kaz let out a moan. From the sounds of it, he might come any second! She plunged her head up and down on his shaft, giving him the most thorough blowjob she could manage. Kaz clung to the bedding and cried out in ecstasy. He gave her a mouthful, but that was okay. A big girl could handle any size load.

"Wow," Kaz said in a daze.

When he fell across the bed, Josie turned to Rob. "Well, he's got that part down."

"Yeah," Rob laughed, beckoning Josie to join him at the head of the bed. "But you know what he's missing?"

"What?"

Rob put on a falsetto voice to whine, "Honey? Honey, don't go to sleep. I'm not done yet."

With a giggle, Josie kissed Rob's neck and nibbled his earlobe. He kissed her shoulder, tracing his fingers down her arm and resting his hand on her hip.

Kicking Kaz in the arm, Rob went on whining, "Honey, finish me off. Pretty-pretty please?"

Kaz didn't respond. He didn't even move.

Josie looked to the silky red corpse at the foot of the bed. "Oh my gosh, we killed him!"

She crawled down to check out the situation. The moment she set her face over his, perfectly prepare to perform CPR, he let out a big honking snore. When she pulled his pyjama pants up to cover his spent cock, he rolled dangerously close to the foot of the bed.

"He's asleep."

"Typical man," Rob replied with a mock-feminine lisp. In his everyday voice, he went on, "Do you think we should carry him up to his room?"

"He isn't Froggy. He's a grown man," she said, lying back with her head on a pillow. "Let's just leave him."

"Well who's going to finish me off now?" Rob asked, returning to his playgirl voice. "A woman has needs, you know. These men think they can use us then throw us out the window like a smoked cigarette. It's just disgraceful."

Shaking her head, Josie chuckled, "You are such a loser."

"Well, that is no way to speak to a lady!"

She leaned over and traced her fingers through the mass of hair around his waiting cock. "How about I pick up where we left off?" she cooed, climbing on board. "Is this okay?"

When she sank her body down on him, they both moaned at that sense complete pleasure, like that first sip of coffee in the morning.

"I guess this'll do," Rob said with a smirk.

She hadn't realized how wet she'd gotten until Rob's cock filled her up. She also hadn't realized how badly she wanted to fuck. Sure it was great to jerk each other off and to suck a few cocks—*had she really done that?*—but, for Josie, no seduction was complete without a cock in a cunt.

She moved on him as he moved in her, playing with her swinging tits. When she leaned forward to wrap her arm around him, she could see the landscape of her body in the dressing mirror.

They both watched as they moved together.

She'd never noticed how hot her ass looked as she teased his cock with broad thrusting motions; she only favoured this position because it made it so easy to rub her clit against him. The mirror leant it a whole new dimension.

They were close enough to kiss, and Rob seemed champing at the bit as she writhed on him. She didn't want him to taste another man's cum on her tongue, but he must have known what he was getting into.

He wrapped his arms around her as she planted her lips on his. He panted and squealed, holding her tight as he thrust in her.

Pressing her clit down hard against his pelvis, she kissed him with the energy of an impending orgasm. Swirling energy, like a galaxy spinning around a black hole. Everything sped up as it reached the event horizon. The faster they moved together, the sooner they would be sucked into the cosmic depths.

It happened. They moaned as their bodies felt lighter, heavier, and larger than life itself.

Josie collapsed on top of Rob. Her thighs ached and her heart beat ten times its normal rate, but she felt fantastic. She probably could have slept like that, but for his sake rolled off to the side.

"Do you think we're weird?" Rob asked.

"No." She could hear Kaz snoring, so it was probably safe to talk about him. "You mean both of us jumping into the sac with someone who's been out of our lives so many years?"

"I don't even remember meeting him," Rob replied, pulling the sheets up and over his waist. "He's just so *cool*, you know? Is it weird for me to think that and be married to you?"

"No," she repeated. "I mean, maybe it's not *usual* to do stuff like this, but maybe it is. I don't know. I only know what goes on in our bedroom, not in anybody else's."

He threw an arm around her. "That's true. But is it bad for *us*, do you think?"

In a sleepy haze, she didn't feel like she could come up with the best of all possible answers. "I think what it shows us is how strong *we* are. We can do all this stuff to help some guy we like and enjoy it and be totally honest about it. The weak couples are the ones who hide it from each other."

"Yeah, you're right," he said in the dark. "It's better to share."

Kaz let out a snort of a snore and rolled toward them.

"He's on my feet."

"Mine too," Rob laughed. "We've got our own human hot water bottle."

Josie took a deep breath, but she knew she wouldn't be able to sleep without asking, "Have you ever done anything like that before? The hot tub, I mean."

Rob didn't say anything right away. She almost said, *never mind, it's none of my business*, but she really wanted to know. Not because it mattered, only because... she was curious.

So she kept her mouth shut until he said, "I guess everybody has."

She didn't want to snap at him, but she'd rather a clear answer than an evasive one. "Does *everybody* include *you?*"

Again, she had to wait for a response. It seemed really bizarre that they could share experiences so easily, but he had such a hard time telling her about stuff that happened before they met. She wouldn't be upset about it.

Finally Rob said, in a bit of a huff, "You know, I feel really used right now."

"Used how?"

They tried to turn and face one another, but their feet were caught under a Japanese guy, so they stared at the ceiling instead.

"I feel like you just want to get off on hearing some story about my youthful indiscretions. Like, *oooh guess what my freak show husband did when he was young?* Those memories are private. I'm sorry."

"You're not ashamed, are you?"

He could have fucked every guy on the football team for all she cared. She would *never* judge him. Though, she couldn't argue that she wasn't fetishizing him. She liked the idea of her husband's younger self giving out blowjobs all around campus. It was *hot*.

"Rob, honey, there's no need to feel embarrassed or guilty or anything. There are as many sexualities as there are individuals. You know I'd never criticize you."

"I know."

When time had passed and he didn't say anything more, she let the issue drop. Everybody had memories they never disclosed to anyone. Josie had memories she didn't even want to let herself remember, like the time her aunt walked in on her masturbating with a yellow zucchini.

God!

She cringed and sent that thought packing. She would never, never tell Rob about that. *Ever*. It wasn't merely the event, but the sense of humiliation that went along with it. She wished she could strip that memory from her neurological make-up.

Maybe that's how Rob felt about whatever it was he wasn't telling her.

Time for sleep.

Chapter Six

When Froggy came rapping at the door early the next morning, Josie pulled her feet out from under Kaz's dead weight. Climbing into the terry robe she'd left lying in a puddle beside the bed, she opened the door and picked up her boy.

"Mommy!" he cheered.

"Froggy!" she cheered back.

He laughed. "Kaz thinks he's a doggie!"

Josie's heart froze as she struggled to understand what he meant. Kaz was sleeping at the foot of their bed. Like a dog.

"Right," Josie laughed. "Do you want to get dressed before or after breakfast?"

"Never!"

Rob shifted in bed, not conscious enough to know what was happening. As he rolled over, his feet launched Kaz clear off the end of the bed.

"Kaz!" Josie cried, setting Froggy down on the carpet. "Are you okay?"

Hopping to his hands and knees, he looked up with a combination of alarm and complete confusion. When he looked around a bit, he seemed to remember where he was, but Josie clarified, "You fell asleep at the foot of our bed, and then you fell on the floor."

"Sorry," he said, quickly rising. "I'll go now."

With a smirk, she said, "Your room's upstairs."

No way he'd remember that on his own.

"Thanks," he replied, stepping between Josie and Froggy to head up to the attic.

Froggy held out his little hand and she took it. Before heading down to the kitchen, she glanced at Rob. She felt like they'd had some sort of disagreement before they fell asleep, but couldn't for the life of her remember what it was about.

"Pancakes?"

"With strawberries!" Froggy replied as he hopped down the stairs.

Rob was the cook of the family, no doubt, but if there was one thing Josie could handle, it was pancakes.

Breakfast was a blast. Rob descended from on high to play his old *Sesame Street Christmas* LP. When Kaz came down, he joined him in acting the record out for the little one at the table. Froggy was over the moon. He jumped up to join them until Josie chuckled, "Come on, you three. Sit down and eat these pancakes I made for you."

They sat like workhorses, but their faces lit up within seconds of placing the fluffy-sweet goodness of her pancakes with pure Quebec maple syrup on their tongues.

"These are delicious," Kaz applauded.

She shot him a Mona Lisa smile. They were straight from a box mix, but nobody needed to know that.

"Mommy makes good pancakes," her son reiterated as Rob cut his up into little pieces.

"What does Daddy make?" Rob asked.

Reflecting intensely while he chewed a slice of banana, Froggy replied, "Good paintings."

The grown-ups laughed. *With* him, not *at* him. Children had an incredible ability to devise unexpected responses to straightforward questions.

"What about you?" Kaz asked. "Are you good at painting too?"

"Yeah," Froggy said. "But Daddy's more better."

Josie smiled at her husband across the table. As they listened with fond appreciation to the record on deck, Kaz asked, "Are you a Froggy like Kermit the Frog? Or like a different kind of frog?"

"Like a frog I catched at the lake," he replied matter-of-factly, but always smiling.

"Ah."

"Yes," Rob cut in. "Froggy spent a week at the lake."

"With cousin Ben," Froggy interrupted.

"With cousin Ben," Rob repeated, sliding his pancake around a pool. "He caught so many frogs that everybody started calling him *Froggy*."

Josie stood to clear some dishes. Better to get out of the house early and back home before the insanity of the Christmas Eve rush took over. "Kaz, we need to go out and buy our Christmas tree this morning."

Froggy leapt on his chair, jumping up and down on the plush seat. "Christmas tree! Christmas tree! Christmas tree!"

Pulling down their son's pyjama top, Rob said, "Sit on your bum and finish your breakfast."

He smiled as he said it, and Josie could see the same excitement in both sets of eyes. In Kaz's too. "You're welcome to come along, if you'd like."

"Thanks," he said with a smile and a nod. As he finished his last sip of tea, a dark look set across his face. "Oh, but I have so much work to finish up before the end of the calendar year. Would you mind if my laptop and I just hung out in your family room for the day?"

Rob whipped his head around quickly, turning his gaze from Froggy to Josie. She wasn't clear what the alarm in his eyes was meant to indicate.

"Yeah, of course you can work here," Josie replied, giving Rob a questioning look.

"What, do you think he's going to steal our silver?" she asked in the bedroom as they changed from pyjamas to tree-shopping attire. They didn't really have time for a conversation. Froggy was already dressed, booted and mittened, and waiting impatiently by the front door. "I really don't understand how you can trust a guy to sleep with us, but not trust him enough to spend the morning in our family room."

Plunging his feet into wool socks, Rob asked, "What if he's nosy? What if he snoops through our stuff?"

"What is there to find? A few silly pictures and a vibrator? Who cares?" She opened the door before he had his pants on, and he hopped around the room, struggling into them. "Come on, let's go. Don't worry so much about things."

As she buckled Froggy into his car seat, she wondered why on earth she felt so irritated with Rob over nothing. It must have been remnants from the previous night, when she wanted so badly to know something and he refused to tell her.

When was it ever a good idea to keep secrets?
Especially secrets the other partner was aware of.
Those ones could haunt even the best of relationships.

Chapter Seven

"I made lunch," Kaz called from the family room as they dragged the tree inside.

Froggy held the top branch, convinced he was doing all the work.

"I hope you don't mind."

"Mind?" Josie cried, bringing up the rear. "Why would we mind? Help yourself to anything. You're our guest."

Rob kicked off his boots and dragged the tree to the front window, clenching his teeth. Kaz better not have gotten into his English fig and walnut jelly. "What did you make?"

"Oh darn!" Josie cried, setting down the tree trunk and slipping out of her snow boots. "I forgot to grab the skirt and base and all that from downstairs. I meant to get that out last night."

As she darted for the basement door, Rob held up the tree with one gloved hand while he tried to unzip Froggy's snowsuit with the other. When Kaz noticed the trouble he was having, he set his computer down and said, "I can give you a hand, if you want."

Letting out a deep breath, Rob replied, "I guess you could help Froggy out of his boots and stuff."

As he watched the care Kaz took interacting with their sleepy son, Rob had to ask himself why he felt so irritated with the guy.

"Thanks, dude," Rob said. "For helping out, I mean."

"No problem, man."

It wasn't Kaz at all, was it? It was the fact that only hours into his stay, Josie was asking about something Rob didn't want to discuss.

Or maybe it *was* about Kaz, but only in the sense that the whole hot tub thing took him back to hurting Faisal. He didn't want to think about that.

Ever.

When Kaz peeled Froggy's snowsuit down over his feet, his son's precious little head fell like a wrecking ball against Kaz's shoulder. Kaz chuckled as Josie's soft footsteps mounted the basement stairs. "I think we've lost him."

When she got to the top of the stairs, Josie cried, "Sorry! This thing was buried under..."

"*Shhh,*" they both hissed. "Froggy's asleep."

"Oh," she said, covering her lips with her fingertips. She chuckled as she caught sight of her boy asleep standing up. "I'll put him down for a nap," she whispered, setting down her huge box of Christmas paraphernalia and scooping the kid into her arms.

When she'd cleared the stairs, Kaz opened the box and pulled out the tree stand. "What is this thing?"

"That's what I put the tree in," Rob replied, pointing in front of the bay window where the base needed to go. "Haven't you ever had a Christmas tree?"

Kaz placed the base on the carpet and then grabbed the tree trunk. "Not a real one. We never really celebrated Christmas when I was a kid. I always wanted to. You know, every December I'd watch all the same Christmas specials on TV that everyone else was watching and I'd be like, *why don't I get a turkey and a tree and a whole bunch of presents?* I was so jealous of all the *normal* families."

"Maybe that's why Josie invited you," Rob proposed. "We're a little disorganized with the tree this year, but we're actually really big on Christmas."

"Yeah, I think that's why she did invite me," he agreed. "A combination of kindness and pity. But, hey, I'll take a real family Christmas. Shelly and I tried to celebrate when we were together, but... I don't know, man. Nothing with us was ever really good. She never seemed like she was happy with me, and I always felt like I was letting her down."

"Shelley was your girlfriend?"

"Yeah, for way longer than she should have been."

When Kaz placed the tree trunk into the base, Rob pushed it upright. The top two feet dragged across the white ceiling so it looked almost like an upside-down L.

"I told her this one was too tall," Rob chuckled, staring at the pine tree kneeling on the ceiling. "Do you want to turn all those wing nuts for me?"

After securing the tree to the base, Kaz stood up, looked up, and laughed his ass off. "What are you going to do about that? Want to snip the tip?"

This guy is awesome! "No, let's leave it for Josie to see. Proves I was right."

"Size matters, man. Even a Christmas tree can be too big."

Rob laughed.

A puzzled look came over Kaz, and he looked around. "Hey, what happened to Josie, anyway?"

"If she went to put Froggy down, ten-to-one odds she fell asleep right beside him."

"Should we wake her for lunch?" Kaz asked, heading to the kitchen like it was his very own foxhole.

"Nah, let her sleep," Rob said with a wave. "She's been working so hard lately. She needs some time to decompress."

Kaz came back out of the kitchen with two plates in hand. "Voilà! Sandwiches and salad. The sleepy-heads will have to get theirs later."

"You made lunch for *us*, you mean?" Rob asked, in awe of the professionally garnished plate in front of him.

"Of course," Kaz replied, heading back into the kitchen only to emerge with two glasses of cranberry juice. "You think I'd just whip up something for myself? I'm not *that* antisocial."

When Rob opened his sandwich to see what was inside, the first thing that caught his eye was the generous dollop of fig and walnut jelly spread across his chicken breast.

Why cry over spilled figs? Life is too short.

He closed the bun and sunk his teeth into the most delicious sandwich ever prepared in his kitchen. "Dude, am I ever glad you're here. This is awesome."

"It's not just a matter of having the right ingredients," Kaz replied. "You have to know how to put them together, you know?"

Yeah.

Chapter Eight

Kaz took his computer to the attic bedroom, sublimely satisfied. He'd done everything he'd seen in every TV special. He decorated a tree alongside a bright-eyed child while two proud parents looked on. He helped Rob prepare a candlelit dinner and drank some ridiculously disgusting eggnog... but, hey, everybody else seemed to like it.

After dinner, he and Josie straightened up the kitchen. Rob and Froggy hung everybody's Christmas stockings on the mantle, then set out milk and cookies for the fat man and carrots for his reindeer. Froggy picked out the perfect cartoon Christmas movie to watch.

After apple cider, pecan pie, and *Charlie Brown Christmas*, Kaz picked up the laptop and headed upstairs. Though Josie, Rob, and even little Froggy all seemed really receptive to his being there, he didn't want to intrude too much. He wasn't familiar with the details of their traditions. Maybe they'd want to do something as a family that didn't involve them.

Even alone in his attic room, Christmas Eve actually meant something to him because he knew he was in a house of love. He could feel it the minute he walked through the door. He could feel it in the way Rob and Josie invited him into their hot tub and into their bed.

Those two had so much love to share that it spilled over the edges of their relationship. He was just lucky to be in a position to get hit with some of the warm excess.

It's not like he anticipated a repeat performance of the previous night, but if they surprised him with something even half as nice, he'd be a happy camper.

He meant to stay up like a child waiting for hooves on the rooftop.

After dressing into his silk pyjamas, he tried to get some work done.

Even with the lights on, he didn't manage to stay awake for long.

AROUND ONE IN THE MORNING, after filling stockings, placing presents beneath the tree, and snacking on cookies and carrots, Josie and Rob slowly opened the door to Kaz's attic room. They weren't sure if they should, without knocking, seeing as his light was still on, but what could he possibly be doing that they couldn't join in?

"Get that computer off his lap," Josie whispered.

Rob was back in his Christmas sleep pants, but she'd squeezed herself into a gorgeous teddy with a wide bow in the middle. He chuckled. "You look like a big red Christmas present."

"I am a Christmas present," she replied as Rob set the computer on the desk. "And excuse me, but what do you mean by *big*?"

"Are you going to wake him up?" Rob asked.

"That *was* the plan."

Kaz moved his head as Josie ran her fingers up the smooth insides of his silk pyjama bottoms. She smiled at Rob when their new friend moaned lightly. His sighs of pleasure made her feel useful, like a goddess of generosity.

With great symmetry and precision, she glided her hands into the red centre of his crotch. There, she found his cock and rubbed it through the silk until it was hard.

"Careful," Rob warned. "You don't want to finish him off before he even knows you've started."

"That's the least of my concerns," Josie whispered, running her fingers down his legs and resting them on his knees. "It's all in his head, the premature ejaculation. His body's fine, it's just anxiety about pleasing a partner."

"Oh, so now you're an expert on urological disorders?"

"I'm telling you, it's all psychological. And what did I say before? Girls know dicks. We really do."

Her whispers roused Kaz.

So did her hands.

He shook his head and squinted like he was trying to figure out who they were.

Then he smiled. "Is it Christmas yet?"

"Technically, yes," Rob said. "Ho ho ho! Merry Christmas!"

"I'm your gift," Josie said, placing her cheek against his thigh and running her hands under his pyjama top.

"I'm your gift too," Rob chimed in.

"Sweet," Kaz said, wiping his eyes. "I've never gotten human gifts before."

"We have an idea," Josie said, running her hands all the way up his chest until they poked through the neck hole of his shirt.

Rob didn't come any closer. Not without specific invitation. "We think maybe it would slow you down if you had something else to concentrate on."

"We want to go all the way with you, Kaz."

"Are you sure?" Kaz asked. "I mean, I'm not very good."

"Don't talk like that," Josie cooed.

How could such a devilishly handsome guy have such low self-esteem? Maybe he was stuck in the mindset of his high school geek self... and maybe getting it on with his high school geek girlfriend would alleviate his apprehensions.

"Here's the idea," Rob began.

With a giggle, Josie picked up, "We think maybe if you were, say, sucking a nice tasty dick while you were getting it on with me, that would distract you just enough to get a few good pumps in. What do you think?"

Kaz's eyes sparkled. He looked from Josie to Rob. "You would do that for me?"

"Sure," Rob chuckled.

"Here, Kaz, get up and we'll show you what we were thinking."

When Kaz scrambled out of the bed, Josie rolled into it. She always did like leaving nice lingerie on—she knew how great she looked in it—so she merely undid the clasps at the crotch of her satin teddy and laid herself out like a sacrificial virgin.

"Wow," Kaz muttered, taking the satin of her bow between his fingers.

With the go-ahead for cock sucking, Rob threw off his pyjama pants and climbed over Josie. He sat his ass down on the thick wood of the headboard so his cock lined up with her body.

"Do you see where you fit in?" he asked Kaz.

"Yeah," Kaz replied without moving. He just stared at Josie.

"Don't be scared," Josie said. She wanted to feel the weight of his body on top of hers. "It isn't as hard as you think."

"Want to get naked?" Rob asked.

"Oh. Right." He slipped out of his pyjama pants and his cock rebounded upwards. When he pulled off his shirt, she could hear Rob panting above her. Maybe he was thinking the same thing. Her breathing patterns had undergone noticeable change as well. "So you just want me to get on top here?"

"Before you do, I want you to feel this." Josie took hold of his fingers. She plunged them into her wet slit so he could feel the juice of her arousal.

His tentative fingers against her pussy lips sent subtle shocks through her, like the gentle paws of a cat walking up her spine.

"How's that?" she asked.

"Nice," he said.

She watched his cock jump as he touched her.

All she wanted was for him to feel happy and confidant.

"Now, why don't you lie down on top of me?" she proposed. "I want to feel that lovely cock of yours right here." She gave her clit a little smack and she liked it. "Not inside, not just yet, but right on top of me."

When she felt his wood against her clit, she immediately pushed her hips forward. She wanted to meet him head-on.

He pressed his cock against her clit and slowly moved his hips. Her temperature rose. Could they call this a dry hump when her pussy was so, so wet?

"That looks awesome," Rob broke in.

Josie scooched back, bringing Kaz with her as she reached up to fondle her husband's cock. Once in hand, it grew big and strong. She stroked it in time with Kaz rubbing his hard shaft along her pussy lips.

When Rob's tip started pumping precum on her tits, that's when she knew it was time to feed the monster to Kaz. She held it by the base as Rob said, "Hey, man, why don't you wrap your lips around this?"

Kaz looked to Josie for instruction, but all she could say was, "Suck it."

So he did. Kaz took Rob's hard cock in his mouth without paying as much attention to his gleaming tip as she would have done. She always liked to lick that ridge, but to each his own. If Kaz wanted to swallow her husband's cock whole, all the power to him.

Anyway, Rob seemed to be enjoying himself.

He grasped the headboard and pressed his body back against the wall. "Oh man, you really know your way around a blowjob."

Josie watched from below as Kaz's pink lips raced along Rob's shaft. At this rate, Rob might even get off before Kaz. He certainly seemed to be reaching the heights of enjoyment.

"Get inside me, Kaz."

Josie plunged her hand between their bodies and took his hard cock in her grip. Even *she* was alarmed by the urgency of her plea. An innocent bystander would have thought she'd die if she didn't get a cock in her cunt. *Stat!*

"Somebody's got a need," Rob laughed.

"Yeah, like you don't," she chuckled, arching her back until she could get the tip of his cock to meet her pussy. "Will this be your first time inside a girl?"

Kaz didn't stop sucking Rob to mumble an affirmation.

She looked past her tits, past her red satin ribbon, and down to the beast waiting at her gate. When he lunged inside her, she felt like someone had taken defibrillator paddles to her chest. She rose upward, until her face was so close to the boys she could nearly lick Rob's balls.

Kaz thrust in her, seemingly without awareness. That's what she and Rob were going for. Distraction. But it surprised Josie that he could move in her so expertly, with such clean thrusts, without paying attention to the fact that they were doing it.

She raised her hips to meet his.

The space between them gave her ample opportunity to watch his cock move toward her, like a rod and piston. How could his motion be so fluid and so mechanical at the same time? He reminded her of a wind-up toy whose movement went on and on while his expression never changed.

At least his movements weren't too jerky.

And at least his expression was blissful as he sucked Rob's cock.

Rob howled at the moon as Josie grabbed Kaz's cute ass. He pumped his hips hard. She wanted to get off. The boys would get off no problem. No way she'd be left out. But how she wished someone would play with her clit. She felt trapped in a cage of men.

She watched as Rob grabbed Kaz's head and fucked it good. Something throbbed in her as her man rammed the guy's throat. The feeling was visceral, and no less real just because it was vicarious.

As she thrust toward Kaz, she envisioned herself shoving a big cock in some guy's mouth, making him suck it, getting her off. She screamed with exhilaration and clenched her pussy muscles, taking control of Kaz.

He yelped like a Chihuahua. She could feel his thighs trembling. She could hear him gurgle as Rob filled his throat with cum.

"Can I take your place?" she asked Rob. After all, he wouldn't need it anymore.

Plunking herself down on the headboard, she instructed Kaz not to fall asleep. "If you want to fuck a girl, you need to stay awake and take care of her after you come."

Kaz sat in front of her on his knees.

"Do you know how to eat a girl?" Rob asked.

With some hesitancy, Kaz replied, "No, not really."

"Oh, man, you need to know how to do that! It's, like, the most important thing there is."

"Well," Josie interrupted. "I'm sure if he can manage to suck a cock, he can do this too. Now, Kaz, I'm already good and warmed up, so you can skip the preliminaries and go straight to sucking my clit."

"That's something that's always confused me," he admitted to Rob.

Opening her pussy lips, Rob pointed out the elusive clit. "Shoot for that, man. You'll never go wrong."

With Rob's face so close to hers, Josie couldn't resist kissing his lips. Kissing was something that had gotten lost when they went into training mode for Kaz.

As they kissed, she felt a face between her legs and light stubble against her thighs. When Kaz sucked her clit, she couldn't believe he'd said he didn't know what he was doing. Sure felt like he did.

Rob reached beneath her teddy to squeeze her tits while Kaz sucked in time with her heartbeat. Two tongues drove her wild. She writhed against Kaz's face. If her mouth weren't occupied kissing her husband, she would have been screaming to the high heavens.

Trapping Kaz's head between her legs, she pressed her pussy against his mouth. Her whole body froze under the suction of his lips. She stiffened and seized until she couldn't hold back. She cried out, "Ooh yeah, baby, yeah that's good!"

The moment her thighs released poor Kaz, he fell into bed. He found sleep the moment his head hit the pillow.

They tucked him in like kindly parents and left him to his dreams.

Josie changed into family-appropriate pyjamas when they got back to their bedroom, but she couldn't fall asleep so easily.

"What did you think of that?" she asked Rob.

"It was great," he said. "Kaz seemed to give you a good minute or two."

"Yeah, I think he did," she replied.

It was hard to measure time fucking. It always seemed to go by too fast.

She thought he might be upset, but she asked anyway, "Have you ever done that before? I mean, had a guy suck your dick?"

"No," Rob said right away. "Nope, never done that before."

That was all the information she needed in that moment, so she let exhaustion catch up with her and fell into sleep.

It seemed like only two minutes later that Froggy was jumping on their bed shrieking, "Santa was here!"

Chapter Nine

"Santa was here! Come look." Froggy took Josie's hand as she sat up in bed. "Come see the presents, Mommy! Make Daddy come, too."

Rob rolled out of bed and made his way to the bathroom. "I'll put some coffee on in a sec. Should we wake Kaz?"

"No, he'll need his sleep," she said as Froggy pulled her by the hand.

Josie wanted to devote the morning to her little boy. The build-up to Christmas had been such a beautiful arc and, as much as she enjoyed Kaz's company, she wanted to stand at its apex with her husband and child.

"Mommy, are these presents all for me?" he asked.

"All for you," she replied.

It warmed her heart that six parcels generated such a glowing response from the boy. If he didn't know other parents spoiled their children with thirty plastic toys, he'd always be happy unwrapping handmade mittens and wooden puzzles fairly traded from Africa.

Picking up a gift from under the tree, he asked, "Does Santa know my name is Froggy now, not Ewan anymore?"

They'd always been amused by the way he pronounced his given name—it came out sounding like *Ewok*.

With a smile, Josie said, "Santa knows everything. Now, let's start with our stockings. We'll unwrap presents when Daddy gets down here."

She wondered what was taking her husband so long as she and Froggy pulled various fruits from their Christmas stockings. Josie never got to meet Rob's parents before they passed, but he remembered them saying all they got in their stockings as children was an apple and an orange if they were good and a lump of coal if they were bad. Rob wanted to carry on that tradition by filling their stocking with fruits.

"Look, Mommy!" Froggy giggled. She wasn't paying attention to what she was pulling out of her stocking; she had both eyes glued to the staircase. "Mommy, you got a lemon!"

"Oh," she replied, looking at the fruit in her hand. "So I did. Well, Mommy likes lemons. She puts them in her ice water and in her hot tea. Lemons are very yummy."

"No, yucky!" Froggy said, squishing up his nose. He held up his fruit. "Pears are yummy."

"Yes, pears are yummy, too," she agreed, leaning forward to see if Rob might be descending the stairs. He wasn't. "Rob, we're opening stockings without you."

"Yeah, Daddy! We started without you," Froggy chimed in, crawling into Josie's lap to sort through the rest of his stocking. "What's this one?"

"That's an apricot. It's like a little peach," she told him as footfalls sounded on the staircase.

"Look who I found," Rob said as he joined them by the fireplace.

A very sleepy Kaz wobbled down the stairs. His eyes lit up like any child's would when he caught sight of the tree and all the presents underneath it.

"There's a stocking for you over here," Rob told him, taking it down from the mantle. On a bit of masking tape, Josie had written "Kaz" to personalize it.

"This is an apricot!" Froggy shouted, holding the little orange fruit in the air.

"Indoor voice," Josie pleaded.

"Oh, coffee," Rob said, hopping over Froggy and Josie to head to the kitchen.

Kaz sat on the floor and dug into his stocking. "Hey, a star fruit. Oh, I recognize this one!"

"What, the persimmon?" Rob called, sticking his head out of the kitchen to see. "Oh, yeah. Josie thought you'd get a kick out of that."

The whirlwind had begun, and Josie rested her back against the ottoman to watch.

Christmas had a circus quality to it, and the only way to both survive and enjoy it was to sit back and observe. She smiled at the familiar joy on Froggy's face, and the novel joy on Kaz's as they sat on the floor eating fruit. She loved Rob, even through the clatter from the kitchen. His need to take care of everyone warmed her heart as her cup of hot coffee warmed her hands. "Thanks, honey."

He kissed her lips softly, and then said, "Should we open presents now?"

"Yeah!" Froggy cried.

He ran to the fragrant tree, followed closely by Kaz and Rob.

Josie wandered over, too, and watched from the sofa as they unwrapped clothing.

When they arrived at the *pièce de resistance*, she joined them on the floor near the tree.

"I think you're really going to like this one," she said as Rob handed him the largest of the gifts.

It was almost as big as Froggy, but he would grow and it would stay the same size.

He tore the paper from his gift in strips from the top down until he'd revealed an object that seemed to both delight and perplex him. Josie picked him up and sat him on the coffee table so he could see the top.

"A drum!" he squealed, clapping his hands above his head.

She pulled it over to him and the moment he could reach it, he tapped the hide with his fingers.

The reverberating sound overwhelmed Josie for a moment. She thought she might cry. "That's a tribal drum, a bongo drum, and it's from far away in Africa."

Standing up on the coffee table, Froggy bent forward to bang on the drum. "Africa!"

"Yes, that's right," she said. "Did you know Mommy's family came from Africa a long, long time ago?"

"Africa! Africa! Bongo, bongo, bongo drum!" Froggy danced and played.

The joy in his face made her smile so wide her jaw hurt. She launched herself at him and took him in her arms with all the love she possessed. "Is this a good Christmas?"

"Yeah, yeah, yeah!" he cried, kissing her cheek.

Rob came close to get his hug and kiss. Judging by the look on his face, she'd guess this was one of Rob's favourite Christmases. He was convinced simple was best.

"I have gifts to give you, if I'm not intruding," Kaz said, collecting wrapping paper from the floor.

"Oh, I'll take those big pieces," Rob offered. "We try to reuse everything we can."

"You shouldn't have bought us anything," Josie told to Kaz.

She meant it, too. They ended up with so much *stuff* over the holiday season just because everybody felt obliged to get them a little something.

As it turned out, that was not the case with Kaz. She'd vastly underestimated his gift-giving abilities.

"Rob and Froggy's gifts I made yesterday," he said, handing a paper box to Froggy. Inside was a whole extended family of brightly coloured origami frogs. "Look at this. If you press on their bums, they hop."

When he demonstrated, Froggy went absolutely wild.

"What a great gift," Rob said, lifting a few frogs onto the bongo drum. Froggy got a kick out of that too. "We're really strong believers in homemade gifts. They're so much more meaningful than plastic stuff."

"I know what you mean," Kaz said, opening his laptop for Rob to have a look. "That's why I decided to make you something too."

"No way, man!"

"Yeah way, man," Kaz teased, opening up a website. *Rob Klimptow Illustrations.* "Remember when we were having pizza the other night, how you were telling me you'd love your own website to showcase your art? Well, here is!"

Rob was visibly astounded. He'd gone into speechless mode. "No way."

"It's no big deal. All I've done so far is the template, which can all be changed if you want, but as soon as you take some digital photos of your work, we can upload them and turn this into the site of your dreams."

Seeing that Rob was at a total loss for words, Josie said, "That looks great, doesn't it, babe?"

"It just..." Rob stammered. He grabbed Kaz's shoulders and squeezed them. "I can't believe anyone would do something like this for me."

Kaz blushed a bit. "Really, it was nothing. It's super, super easy to throw a website like this together. And the best part is there are no hosting fees or anything to worry about."

When Rob threw himself at Kaz to give the guy a heartfelt hug, Froggy quickly followed suit, and Josie rushed to get his precious computer off his lap.

"Did you open yours yet?" he asked her from under the assault of affection.

"Oh, no," she replied. She'd put the box down to watch Froggy open his origami frogs. When she cracked open the hinges on her wooden box, she found inside a beautiful necklace made of mauve-coloured freshwater pearls. "Oh, Kaz, this is gorgeous."

"*That* I don't claim to have made," he said as she fitted the pearls around her neck. She couldn't believe he remembered her favourite colour from back then. "I actually bought that from Shelley. You know, to stay on good terms. She makes jewellery, and I didn't want to pick up random department store crap for your family."

He stood up, glowing, when she went over to give him a hug. "These are beautiful gifts. Thank you so much."

Just as he said, "I wanted to show you how much I appreciate your hospitality," the front door burst open.

Chapter Ten

In walked a group of people Kaz hadn't seen since he and Josie were an item.

"Merry Christmas! Where's my little grandson got to?"

"Mamma!" Froggy shrieked, running over to Winnie. She picked him up and twirled him around in the air.

"Merry Christmas, Mom," Josie said. "Kaz, you remember my mom, Winnie." Glancing behind her, she said to her sister and nephew, "And Vivian and Nathan, take your boots off and come on in, you two. Do you remember my boyfriend Kaz?"

"Now you got a husband and a boyfriend?" Nathan teased. "That must keep you busy, Auntie Josie."

"My boyfriend from high school," she clarified, shooting a smile at Rob. He'd turned away from her to talk to her mom, so she gave the smile to Kaz instead.

There was so much family in the room, and none of it his. Kaz wasn't sure if he should hide behind the couch, retreat to the kitchen, or try to blend in. "I can't believe this is the same Nathan. I remember you when you weren't much bigger than Froggy!" Hearing the words that had just passed through his lips, Kaz covered his forehead with his hand. "Sorry, I'm starting to sound like an old man, aren't I?"

"Aren't you an old man?" Nathan quipped, taking a seat on the sofa.

"Nathan, mind your manners," Vivian scolded her son. She looked Kaz up and down, and he couldn't believe this was the same Vivian.

Vivian the drop-out, the stereotype, the bad girl. She seemed so well put together now, in an embroidered silk brocade top and elegant black trousers. He felt embarrassed to still be wearing pyjamas, even though Josie, Rob, and Froggy were still in theirs.

Sure, Vivian had always been pretty, but the beauty she shared with Josie used to be hidden under layers of cheap make-up and clothing. Now her beauty was the first thing he saw. There was no need to dig for it anymore.

"Are you sure you're the same boy our Josie went with in high school?" Vivian asked, extending her hand to shake his.

"Yup, same guy, just a few years older."

Once she had his hand in hers, she seemed to change her mind. She gave him a big hug instead. "I just don't believe it. I remember you as a science geek."

Nathan laughed from the sofa, smacking his knee.

"I *was* a science geek," Kaz said.

"Maybe you ought to sit down next my son so some'll rub off on him," she chuckled.

"Hey Vivian," Rob called from across the room, where he and Winnie were admiring the new drum. "Ask Kaz to show you the website he made me. It's great."

"You're not a web designer," Vivian said, smacking him on the shoulder. "I'm doing graphic design now. Isn't that far out!"

"Are you really? That's great."

"Show him your card, Mom," Nathan offered. "You should see her work, man. My mom gets some serious respect."

Kaz took one look at Vivian's business card and laughed. "You're *Slippery When Wet Designs*? I'm *Thundershore*! This is unbelievable." He looked around for someone to tell, but everyone else was busy banging on the bongo, so he said to Nathan, "We chat online, like, every day."

"I can't believe it's you," she said, giving him another hug. "Nathan, he's Thundershore. How about that!"

"That's crazy," her son said, getting up from the sofa to shake his hand. "I really respect your designs, man. My mom talks about you all the time."

"I wondered why you hadn't been online much," Vivian went on. She held the sleeves of his pyjama top and wouldn't let go. "It's because you've been right here at my little baby sister's house. That's just incredible."

"Yeah, I know," Kaz admitted, looking over at Froggy as he unwrapped his grandma-gifts. "I've really missed chatting."

"Me too."

"Me too," Nathan imitated, speaking in falsetto and fluttering his eyelashes.

Vivian shook her head, smiling at her son. "Show us this website Rob was talking about."

"Oh, it's nothing," he replied, sitting down with the two of them and opening his laptop. "I should be asking you for help, Slip. Sorry, *Vivian*. I'll have to get in the habit of calling you by your real name now."

FROM ACROSS THE ROOM, Josie watched Kaz with her big sister and her eldest nephew as they brainstormed design possibilities. With smiles that wide it was a wonder their faces didn't crack.

As she pressed her fingers against her cool coffee mug, she decided her bitterness was nothing more than hunger pains. She'd feel better once she'd eaten something. Really, it was wonderful that Kaz seemed to be hitting it off with Vivian. They'd both been unlucky in love. If they could be happy together, she'd be happy too.

Christmas dinner turned into even more of a whirlwind, but she should hardly have been surprised. Family events were like that. There was so much activity it was impossible to keep track of what everyone was up to.

Adrianna prepared a gorgeous meal that spoke even to the demanding palates of her husband and Kaz, though Kaz would likely have been content with beans on toast as long as he was sitting at Vivian's side.

Why am I getting so worked up about this?

She ought to be over the moon for the pair. There was something tremendously serendipitous about meeting someone in one context, and then finding them again in another. It was the Fates screaming, "Didn't you get it the first time, dummy? You're supposed to be together!"

As she sliced her perfectly moist turkey and topped it with cranberry sauce and almond stuffing, she watched Vivian set her hand on Kaz's. She chewed so hard she could feel her teeth grinding together.

So, why am I watching if it just gets me upset?

Josie turned her head to watch Froggy and his cousin Ben, but Rob caught her eye first. It was embarrassing. He could obviously see her upset; he was good with stuff like that.

She didn't want to feel jealous. It was Christmas; she should feel jolly.

"Did your wife go into a coma?" Adrianna's husband asked hers.

"Huh? What's that?" Josie replied. "What did I do?"

Rob smiled meekly. "Adrianna just asked if Froggy could stay overnight with Ben."

"You want to spend your Christmas night at Auntie Adrianna's, not at home with Mommy?"

"Yeah," Froggy cheered, standing up on his chair. "Stay here with cousin Ben."

"Come on, sit down on your bum," Rob instructed.

That was the last thing she heard clearly before the cacophony of dinner noises took over. She could feel hot tears welling in her eyes. She didn't want to cry, but that didn't seem to matter. Pushing back her chair, she swept out of the kitchen and down to the front door.

She slipped on her snow boots and winter coat, and went outside.

Josie wasn't sure where to go once she'd stepped out onto the porch, so she brushed some snow off the patio swing and sat down. It was nice to be able to see stars, even if it was only seven in the evening. Winter had its pros and cons. She tried only to see the pros: the freshness in the air, the reflection of dark blue skies on pristine snow, Christmas...

When she heard the screen door squeal, she knew it was Rob. She didn't need to look. He'd come armed with a blanket, as it turned out.

When he sat down beside her and spread it over their legs, she leaned her head on his shoulder and sighed.

"Nobody needs me anymore."

He chuckled. "Try *everybody needs you always*."

"Kaz has Vivian, Froggy has Ben..."

"And you have me." He kissed her hair.

"That's true," she said, reflecting on everything she might get out of the moment. "Why won't you tell me about what you did?"

"What I did when?"

"I don't know," she said. "In university, I guess. Whatever you wouldn't tell me the other day."

She could feel his body stiffen next to hers. "Do we really have to go down this road? Do we both have to be upset? It's Christmas."

"So make it my Christmas present," she begged. Recalling the yellow zucchini, she lied, "You know everything about me. I hate thinking there's something you're hiding."

"It was Faisal," he said, almost before she'd finished speaking. "It was Faisal."

"Was he at our wedding?"

"Yeah, we were really good close friends when we were younger," Rob began, pulling her in close.

Rob was always so warm. He was the perfect man to sit next to on a crisp winter's evening.

"When you're a young man, you know, you have all these hormones and you do things sometimes that you're ashamed of later on."

"Rob," she interrupted. "What, you got each other off? So what? There's nothing to be ashamed of there."

"I know," Rob replied, taking a long pause. "It wasn't that. I mean, yeah we did, and I guess I found it thrilling and necessary and shameful all at once. We were young."

"I know."

Zucchini.

"There was almost a ritual to the whole thing. We depended on each other, in a sense. And then one day Faisal came out with this statement that he..."

After a moment of suspense, she asked, "He had a girlfriend?"

"No, he was in love with me," Rob said. He seemed to laugh and moan at once. It was a haunting sound.

"Oh," Josie replied. She thought that was the sweetest thing she'd ever heard, but Rob didn't seem to agree. "Sex is like that. We think we can get off with just anybody and it doesn't have to mean anything, but, you know, it does mean something. Every time."

"I was so angry," Rob went on. "I chewed him out*: this is not love, I am not gay, get your filthy hands off me*. He begged. He said how much courage it had taken him to tell me. His parents would disown him if they found out, but he would make any sacrifice for me. And I had these images of his father coming after me with a machete, like, *You are the boy who corrupted my son! You must die!* Faisal pleaded with me and I got so angry."

"Oh sweety," she consoled, hugging him around his waist. "We all make mistakes growing up. We all do these things."

"I know, but Faisal..." He stopped, and when he sniffled she knew he was holding back tears. "I wouldn't talk to him, wouldn't look at him. I had no sympathy. He was this smart,

smart guy and he ended up staying an extra year at school and it was all because of me."

"Oh, Rob," she cried, hugging him tight just to keep him in one piece. She'd done stupid things in life, but nothing that generated the kind of remorse Rob had hidden all through the years. "You never told me any of this."

"I thought you'd hate me."

"I could never hate you," she said, kissing his cheek. "I love you for sharing."

"But don't you think I'm in total denial or something? Don't you think..."

"I've always been of that school of thought that says there are as many sexualities as there are individuals," Josie began. "We all have our attractions, we all have our crushes, and some of us are lucky enough to have life-long crushes on the people we marry. That's how I feel about you. I love you, I like you, and I have a huge crush on you that won't go away."

Rob smiled at that. "Yeah, I know what you mean. So you don't hate me for the way I acted when I was young?"

"I didn't even know you then," she said, kissing his cold nose. "I love you for who you are now, and the respect you show me and our child."

She was about to suggest they head back inside when Rob asked, "What do we do about Kaz?"

Her heart sank a little at the mention of his name. "What do you mean?"

"Well, you just said sex always means something even when we convince ourselves it doesn't. What do you think is going to happen for us if we let Kaz ride off into the sunset without any closure?"

"Ride off on Vivian?" she spat.

"See what I mean?"

She took a deep breath to keep her emotions in check.

"You're right," she agreed. No use denying it. "Well, Froggy's staying with Adrianna tonight. How about you and I bring Kaz home with us and have some adults-only closure?"

With a deep chuckle, Rob kissed her lips. Their breath mingled like smoke on the cool breeze.

Chapter Eleven

Rob pushed back the coffee table and unfolded a fleece throw on the carpet while Josie lit candles all around the room. Kaz turned the Christmas tree lights on and the house lights off.

The fireplace was gas, but it was better than nothing. It added to the room's sexual ambiance.

"Did you lock the door?" Rob asked. "We don't want your mother walking in while we're in the middle of this."

"Yeah, I got it," Josie chuckled, tearing out of her dinner clothes and dropping them on the floor.

Rob picked them up and folded them with his own on the armchair.

Kaz added to the pile.

"That was a great dinner," he said, sitting cross-legged on the throw.

"Yeah, it was nice not to have to worry about all the prep work for once," Rob agreed, sitting beside him.

"Adrianna always was the cook of the family," Josie said, completing their circular triangle. "So, here we all are."

"Yup," Kaz agreed, nodding his head.

"Let's hold hands," Josie suggested.

"And sing Kumbaya?" Rob teased, taking her hand and Kaz's.

Josie could feel herself blushing. It *was* a little campy, but it felt right. "I just want to take this one a little seriously. After all, it's Christmas. Can we start by just saying a few words?"

"Like a prayer?" Kaz asked. "Sorry, I don't know your traditions."

"No," Josie began, but she wasn't sure how to explain what she was after, so she just said, "I felt jealous today, watching you and Vivian together."

"Oh."

Rob squeezed her hand for support. The central heating must have switched on, because she could feel warm air along her back. "And I know it's not my place to be jealous, but I think that's what happens when we go into sex thinking it won't affect us. That's when it affects us most. So this time I want to go into this with my heart on my sleeve. I'm so glad you could join us for Christmas, Kaz. I'm glad Rob and I could show you the ropes, in a sense, and I'll be happy for you and Vivian if everything works out."

"Thanks," Kaz said, running his hand along her forearm. "I want to thank you both for the confidence you've given me over the past couple days. If it weren't for you guys, I would totally have shied off Vivian in person, even though we've come to know each other so well online. Josie, I always wanted you to be my first, and you were. Now I think I can move on and really know that I can please a woman. It takes practise, like anything else, but you two have given me the confidence to just go with it."

"I'm really glad about that," Rob said. "And a lot of good has come out of this for me, too. Josie got to asking about something in my past that I'd been really ashamed of. I never realized how good it could feel to just tell somebody about it. Yeah, I still don't feel good about the whole thing, but now instead of keeping all that shame to myself I get to share it with my best and closest friend."

Josie squeezed his hand, gazing with admiration down his jaw line, back up around his chin and past his nose. When his gaze met hers, her heart skipped and she squeezed his hand again. Rob and Kaz were a couple of the sweetest guys on the planet.

She laughed. "I can't believe I'm teaching you how to have sex so you can do it with my sister."

"Let's not think about that," said Rob. "Let's just say it's a life lesson."

"You know what I realized?" Josie said to Kaz. "Aside from oral sex, we haven't really shown you how to warm a girl up. It's really important that you do."

"Yeah, girls are a lot like cars," Rob said in absolute earnest.

Josie laughed. "No, we're not. But the thing you want to remember is that girls get our erections on the inside."

"Do you really?" Rob asked.

She shook her head. "My husband doesn't even know these things. Yes, when we get aroused our pussies get bigger just like your dicks do. Did you really not know that?"

"No," Rob said with a shrug. "Man, you should have your own TV show or something."

Kaz smiled at them both. "So what do you think is the best way to warm up?"

"Oh, I know the answer to this one!" Rob cried. Leaning in close, he planted his lips on Josie's and kissed her with a smooth sort of desperation.

A wave of warmth ran through her, and it was more than just air from the heating vent this time. She felt her nipples tighten to buds as he pressed them between his fingers. Her pussy wanted attention, but Rob surprised her by giving Kaz an unexpected instruction.

As Rob kissed her lips, another tongue kissed her far, far below.

As far down as possible, in fact.

Kaz took her toes into his warm mouth and her spirit nearly leapt from her body. Rob had to hold her down to keep her from kicking anybody.

The sensation of tongue on toes was so divinely pleasurable she could hardly bear it.

Breaking away from Rob's kiss, she cried, "Mother of Christmas, that's good!" Her body jerked every which way, and though Rob tried to keep her still, he couldn't manage it. She bucked into the air and side to side. "Oh Kaz, I'm going to have a heart attack if you don't stop."

He gave her one last lick and dropped her foot in his lap. "Did you just have an orgasm?"

"You know, I think I did."

"Wow," Rob cheered. "That worked even better than I thought it would. I can't believe you had an orgasm just from getting your toes sucked."

Like a puddle in the middle of the carpet, she replied, "I know, but it feels really good. I mean, *really* good."

Kaz and Rob looked blankly at one another for a moment before they both started laughing.

"Come on, guys. Don't laugh, just do it." They both smiled, but it took Josie saying, "Okay, how about a toe-sucking daisy chain?" for them to go for it. "Rob, you suck mine, I suck Kaz's, and Kaz sucks yours. Sound good?"

Back in circle formation, she took Kaz's long and straight toes in her mouth and he nearly exploded. "*That*'s what that feels like?"

He took in Rob's toes and his face lit up like a carnival game. "Why have we never done this before?"

When Rob wrapped his tongue around her toes, she nearly bounced off the ceiling. She couldn't conceive of any other sensation that felt so immediately orgasmic. In under a minute, she was desperate for a good fuck. "Who's going to do me, guys? I need it *now*!"

"Start with Kaz," Rob said, obviously hoping Kaz wouldn't last too long.

"Yeah, start with me!"

"Get on your back," Josie instructed, crawling over to him and climbing on board. Rob got in behind her, taking her tits in his hands as she grabbed Kaz's cock by the base. "Tell me what you're thinking."

"I'm thinking I hope I don't come in your hands."

Rob laughed behind her. "Something better than that. Something with the words *gorgeous, sexy*, or *beautiful*."

"I concur," Josie said with a nod.

"Okay," Kaz replied, preparing to try again. "Josie, you were the sexiest, most gorgeously beautiful girl at our high school."

"That's a little better," Rob said.

"Well, it's good enough," she told him. "I'm horny as hell! I need this dick inside me."

When she fell on his cock, they both gasped. It felt huge inside her, like it opened her right up.

Rob squeezed her tits, kissing her back as she rocked on Kaz's cock.

"You know what I'd really like?" she asked, rising and falling on him.

"I think I do," Rob replied, reaching for the toy they'd brought from upstairs.

When he turned it on and buzzed the vibe against her clit, she had to grab hold of Kaz's outstretched arms.

"You like that, do you?" Rob teased, holding her around the waist as he moved the little vibe against her clit.

"You... know... I... do," she panted, throwing herself on Kaz's cock.

He stared up at her, in a total daze.

She worked him so fast she could hardly feel her thighs.

"This is hard!" she said with a breathy laugh.

Handing the vibe to Kaz, Rob said, "You take over with this. Remember, you can't just lie back and do nothing. You should always be playing with her clit or her tits or even just bouncing her hips like this." Taking hold of her waist, Rob lifted her and dropped her back down on his cock.

She felt like a rag doll.

It didn't take long for Kaz to get curious about the vibe, and it didn't take long after shifting the vibe down to the base of his cock for him to start moaning and bucking at her. His cock felt so deep inside her, she doubted it would ever find its way out.

There was so much going on in and around her she could hardly breathe. Rob dropped her to take hold of her tits while Kaz moved his furious cock inside her.

They watched as he arched his back and gritted his teeth.

They watched him stress and strain, and then release and drop back down to the floor.

Josie felt Kaz's muscles relax as his eyes fluttered shut.

"I think we've lost him," she said to Rob, trying to catch her breath. "He's really got to break this habit."

"Come on. Let him sleep," Rob said, taking her by the hand. He led her to the sofa and laid her down, with her head on a throw cushion. "Comfy?"

"Oh yes," she replied as he ran a stream of kissed between her breasts and down her belly.

When he arrived at her pussy, he licked it clean.

Jumping under the fury of his tongue, she cooed, "You love the taste of another man's cum, don't you babe?"

"Mmm-hmm," he replied, with his mouth on her clit. Climbing up her body, he kissed her tits. "But there's nothing I love more than you."

She smiled tenderly as he pushed his cock inside her. She gasped, but didn't say anything. Looking around the room, at the soft lights of candles and the glowing Christmas tree, her heart overflowed with the joy.

Not many women had husbands like hers.

She could feel his cock inside her, moving as they writhed in unison.

As she wrapped her arms around her husband, she suddenly realized Kaz was sitting on the coffee table.

He was holding their little vibrator.

Josie smiled and pointed. "Use the lube."

Rob didn't know what hit him when Kaz eased the vibrator into his ass. She felt his chest bounce on hers with the shock of being penetrated.

"Fuck my husband," Josie purred.

"With the vibe?"

"With your dick."

She loved how dirty it sounded. She loved how the *k* sound popped in her mouth as she said it.

Dick.

Rob didn't say anything in response, so she figured he must be into it.

Kaz chuckled nervously. "I don't know. I need some recovery time."

"No you don't," Josie scoffed. "Come, put your dick in my mouth. I'll show you how hard you can be."

He did as he was told, and she sucked his limp cock until it grew hard and thick. Rob kept right on fucking her as she treated Kaz to a supremely effective blowjob.

"How's that?" she asked, full with pride. "Now are you ready to fuck my husband? Use the lube, remember."

"I know," Kaz replied, picking up the bottle.

Josie asked, "And you, my love? Are you ready for this?"

Rob growled, fucking her in double time until Kaz climbed on board.

Then he slowed to a crawl, until he stopped thrusting altogether.

He dropped his weight on her, his cock in her cunt, while Kaz penetrated his ass.

Josie could feel when he was inside by the way Rob squeezed her.

He felt her breasts and kissed her neck as Kaz rocked in him.

"I can't believe how tight your asshole is."

Letting out a loud moan, Rob tensed up, then relaxed.

"Did you come in me?" Josie asked.

"Yeah," Rob replied. "Virgins come fast."

"Want me to keep going?" Kaz asked.

"Yes," they both shouted.

So he rocked in Rob's ass.

Josie watched over her husband's shoulder as Kaz pulled out, then ran his cock down the crack. He coated Rob's hole with lube, then forced his way inside again.

She could have sworn she felt her man's cock jerk inside her cunt, even after he'd come.

"How does that feel?" she whispered in Rob's ear as Kaz rode him a little faster. The motion felt incredible, even to her on the bottom.

"Oh," he moaned, at a loss for words. "So good."

"Yeah?" she asked. She loved the look of Kaz's hands on her husband's butt cheeks, and of the dark fuzz around his cock as he rammed her husband's hole. "You like getting fucked up the ass, do you?"

"Oh, yes."

As Kaz kept at it, she asked, "What does it feel like for you?"

He moaned.

So did Rob.

"It's like fucking an impossibly tight hole," Kaz cried, lunging at Rob. "Man, he is so tight. So tight, so tight."

His veined forearms shook. When he threw his head back, his ecstatic mouth fell wide open. He didn't make a sound, only held that pose with his back arched and his cock in Rob's ass.

Depleted, he fell forward.

The pressure was nothing short of wonderful.

Collectively, they formed a drained, wet, panting heap.

That unassailable ogre called Exhaustion took over.
Warmth wrapped them in a loving blanket.
Limbs grew heavy.
Breaths grew deep.
Eyes closed.

Chapter Twelve

They slept until the wee hours of the morning, when Josie awoke in a jolt of panic. Why all the lit candles? And naked men?

Where was Froggy?

Sleeping at his cousin's house.

The naked bodies belonged to Kaz and her husband.

They had a threesome last night.

Josie smiled. As she writhed beneath the male bodies, they rose like zombies from the sofa. They weren't even awake, as far as she could tell.

They stood naked, chest to chest, and kissed in their sleep.

She watched as Kaz slipped a weighted arm over Rob's shoulder. Their sleepy lips met and retreated, making faint smacking sounds.

When the motion ceased, she blew out the candles.

In darkness, they moved slowly toward the stairs, inching upwards and forwards until they found a big bed to sleep in.

Vivian and Kaz had agreed to go to the zoo on Boxing Day, but by the time morning rolled around, their intimate date had grown into a family affair.

Not only did Nathan invite himself along as a chaperone, but Froggy and cousin Ben decided they were coming too, which meant they needed supervision. Since Josie's mom hadn't been to the zoo in a good twenty years, she decided to go as well.

Over breakfast, Josie shot Kaz a complicit smile as the whole family rushed in the front door. Soon the kids were banging the drum and her mom was dancing around the room with her favourite sons-in-law.

If they were going to the zoo, they shouldn't leave it too late in the day, Vivian warned, but since no one seemed to be listening to her, Josie advised that she and Kaz take off on their own. The rest of the family would meet up with them later, but at least they'd get a few minutes to themselves.

"You don't mind this?" Vivian asked Josie. "After all, he was *your* boyfriend first."

"Yeah," Josie said with a shrug. "He was, but that was a long time ago. Now I've got Rob. Besides, you and Kaz have so much in common. It was meant to be."

They snuck out in Vivian's car and headed off to spend time alone.

Families were the lifeblood of society, but sometimes they couldn't seem to tell when their members needed a little time off.

When Josie sat down to her toast and coffee, Rob came over to join her. The look of elation in his eyes said everything he couldn't.

The experience they'd shared with Kaz brought them closer together in so many ways. They always knew they had a strong bond, but they'd never imagined it was strong enough to support other people. It seemed unbelievable that bringing a third into their bed could actually fuse their relationship.

And the secrets...

“Rob,” Josie began, tapping her toast against her plate. “There’s something I have to tell you.”

He gripped her arm warmly. “What’s up, hon?”

She could hardly hear herself think through the familial cacophony. She leaned in and spoke right into his ear. “I need to tell you about the yellow zucchini...”

ABOUT GISELLE RENARDE

Giselle Renarde is an award-winning queer Canadian writer. She was nominated Toronto's Best Author in NOW Magazine's 2015 Readers' Choice Awards, and her book The Red Satin Collection won Best Transgender Romance in the 2012 Rainbow Awards. Giselle has contributed erotica and queer fiction to more than 100 short story anthologies, including Best Women's Erotica, Best Lesbian Erotica, Best Bondage Erotica, and Best Lesbian Romance. She's written dozens of juicy books, including Anonymous, Seven Kisses, Bali Nights, Ondine, and Nanny State. Giselle lives across from a park with two bilingual cats who sleep on her head.

Want to stay up to date? Visit
http://donutsdesires.blogspot.com[1]!
Sign up for Giselle's newsletter: http://eepurl.com/R4b11

1. http://donutsdesires.blogspot.com/

You might also enjoy:

Anonymous

An Erotic Novel

By Giselle Renarde

WHAT KIND OF WIFE DREAMS of watching her husband with another man?

A wife like Hannah.

For years, she and Nathaniel have fantasized about bringing a third into the bedroom. But what if it doesn't work out? Could spell disaster for everyone involved.

That's why Hannah and Nathaniel need a hired hand. Someone... anonymous.

Will a night of ménage with a mystery man satisfy their desires? Or will Hannah become so obsessed with discovering the true identity of Mr. Anonymous that she doesn't even realize her husband is falling for someone much closer to home?

Find Anonymous at your favourite ebook retailer!

Also available in print and as an audiobook!

www.ingramcontent.com/pod-product-compliance
Ingram Content Group UK Ltd.
Pitfield, Milton Keynes, MK11 3LW, UK
UKHW021647190726
13853UKWH00001B/106